The Journeys of Hamlin Baylis Wells

Also by Ray Clift and published by Ginninderra Press

Fiction

The Journey of Hamlyn Baylis Wells

Always In Denial

Smithy's Cupboard

Shaken & Stirred

Shalom Samuel

The Last Journey of Hamlin Baylis Wells

She Walks the Line

Non-fiction

Maybe Blue Ghosts

It's a Fine Line

Cops, Crooks, Courts & Spooks

Ray Clift

The Journeys
of Hamlin Baylis Wells

The Journeys of Hamlin Baylis Wells
ISBN 978 1 74027 960 4
Copyright text © Ray Clift 2015
Cover: Gary MacRae

First published separately as *The Journey of Hamlin Baylis Wells* 2009
and *The Last Journey of Hamlin Baylis Wells* 2013

This edition published 2015 by
GINNINDERRA PRESS
PO Box 3461 Port Adelaide SA 5015
www.ginninderrapress.com.au

Contents

The First Journey

Prologue

The fifty-year-old Victoria Police detective was seated in accordance with the rules of undercover duty, on the left-side front seat of an older model VN Commodore sedan. It was a foggy, damp night in the winter of 1996 in Melbourne. A good night for covert duties in the suburb of Brunswick.

Throughout the long shift, with comfort breaks designated by the rule book, he would make notes of the comings and goings of vehicles and people, to and from the house of interest. As the dark approached, he would use a pencil light to assist in recording those vital notes, creating a narrative of the two-storey house and its bare Tuscan-style of building which was recently becoming fashionable.

Hamlin Wells was always called Holy, a nickname foisted on the meticulous man many years ago. The apt title, which referred to his Catholic upbringing, was a signal to any newcomers: Hamlin was not a bender of rules. Over the years he had tried to distance himself from the label but it had adhered to him like correction fluid spilled on fingers. His seniors concluded he had served the state well; he had numerous mentions for bravery and a highly developed sense of right and wrong. He was rated highly.

His unblemished record of service was drawing to a close. Hamlin had indicated it was time for a change – either to retire and take a lump sum, or to return to normal plainclothes duties. His term of service in covert duties had officially expired some five years previously and yearly psychological tests were conducted.

His boss almost begged for his best operative to remain covert. His last assessment seemed normal but the medico had scrawled at the end of the text, 'dissonance'. Hamlin's boss glossed over the word, choosing not to look in a dictionary. The medico had known for sometime that his subject was wearing a mask. Hamlin was able to emotionally pretend all was well when in fact he frequently experienced an opposite emotion.

The nature of covert work required a complete focus on the task and distracting thoughts were not helpful. But Hamlin was distracted. His marriage was in its last stages. Hamlin knew his magician act would not last. He asked God to keep him focused for a few more months. He did not wish to run out of petrol yet. Still, walking out from under the blanket of security which had sustained him in those nearly thirty years would be hard.

He contemplated the decline of his marriage, both of them powerless to stop the slide, Debbie walking away, no kids. The signs had been there for some time. Debbie drifting away into some interior, inaccessible place.

A cold chill came across him. He was not able to shut out the biting cold. Not able to turn on the broken barely working fan which sounded like a World War II bomber deliberately fashioned to frighten a population. Already huddled in fear, Hamlin pulled a blanket over his body, on top of the old duffel coat loosely thrown over the combat jacket acquired in his war service. It gave him the appearance of the Michelin man.

His discomfort was forgotten when he heard the sound of sirens approaching. He sat up, wide awake now. Hands out of pockets. Senses on red alert.

A car turned into the street slightly ahead, moving slowly. It was an unmarked police vehicle with two plain clothes detectives. A spotlight was being swung around, its beam searching. Looking for something.

'Holy hell,' Hamlin said to himself. The target must be near… The adrenalin if they found him, like gold fossickers finding a nugget, wiping it and the yellow colour appearing. Hamlin owned a metal detector and knew the rush of excitement. The car moving, still crawling slowly like a lioness on all fours.

A movement from behind and a dark-clad figure emerged, wearing a dark top coat, crossing the road. Rapidly. The figure halted near the high wall of the property which Hamlin was watching. The man reached under his coat and produced a case. Looking over the wall, he carefully placed the case down and moved away, slipping into the shadows of the oppressive atmosphere.

Hamlin noted the time – 22.30 hours. Soon time to return to the station. In that moment an instant impulse entered his mind. He alighted, moving across the road, diagonally, casually. He reached over the wall and saw a gleaming chrome handle. Plucking the case out of its hiding place, he made his way back to the car, started it and moved off.

He parked near a vacant allotment, some kilometres away, opened the case and then quickly closed it. Slowly reopening it, he saw fifty-dollar bills neatly tied up. He estimated at least seven hundred thousand dollars. 'I'll log in and tell them I'm leaving my location. Park at the station…put the case in the boot of my car. I'll admit if I'm asked that I heard sirens, saw the police searching.'

After calling in and receiving the communications centre's reply, 'Roger', Hamlin drove back, carefully, contemplating the enormity of his actions in deciding not to hand the money in. Fidgety now like a traffic duty cop with piles and his conscience now awoken, he asked himself, 'Should I hand it in? No one'll come forward to claim it. What would happen to it if I did hand it in? Probably be swallowed up in government coffers. I'd do good with it.'

Detective Sergeant Ted Edwards spoke first, eyeing his old mate, his church-going friend, with the quizzical look which always marked him out. 'How's the missus going, Holy?'

'Gone is the operative word, Ted.'

Concerned about his old friend, Ted said, 'Take some time off, Holy. You look like a man who just ran a marathon without shoelaces.'

Hamlin managed a grin and was about to reply when Ted held up his hand. Cocking his right ear to a police handset, he said, 'Shit, mate, you were in Brunswick tonight watching that place, weren't you?'

'Yeah. What's up?'

'What time did you leave?'

'Ten-thirty-five, Ted. I radioed in.'

'Guess what. There was a home invasion. Two blokes dead. Hold it, I'll contact Major Crime and dig some more.' Ted rang a number and scribbled on a pad. 'Holy, listen to this. It appears that a dealer running away from our D car evaded them. Must have had something else on his mind He banged on Bryant's door. No response and then chucks a brick through the front window, clambers in armed, seen by a passer-by. He's met by Bryant, who lets off both barrels and at the same time the dude shoots. Both dead. Scratch two drug dealers. Can't say I'm sorry.'

Hamlin said, 'I heard sirens and saw a car shining spotlights.'

'Get me a copy of your log, mate, in case Major Crime want it.'

Hamlin drove home. After counting the seven hundred and fifty thousand dollars, he did not sleep. He prayed to God for guidance and vowed to perform good deeds with the money.

1

Hamlin Baylis Wells had gathered scars all his life in the service of his highly evolved conscience. He never pinched other children's toys, never hid the wonderful biscuits his mother made, unlike his younger sister Angela, who was never one to give away what she had acquired. It occurred to him as he grew older that she was just a hoarder.

The only items he kept from his mother were brussels sprouts, not out of secrecy – he just hated the smell. She tracked the rotting smell, discovering the source behind his wardrobe. At least six yellow items were removed and buried in the backyard while Hamlin watched, fearfully, expecting some recrimination. Yet none came. The lesson shaped the young boy's picture of Hell: a picture not of fire, but of being attacked by brussels sprouts. Giant sprouts with eyes and a much more frightening mouth. The dreams lingered for years, recurring like an irritating TV commercial.

At ten he became a paper boy, and gave all his money to his mother. The list of his sins was diminishing. Those sins which accumulated during the passing of a day were soon expunged in his nightly prayer to God

His God-fearing parents relied on their weekly chat to the priest, which sustained them for the coming week. Hamlin loved the time, considering it had moulded him in many aspects, and later in his studies he concluded it had been free therapy, a cheap form of non-directive counselling. Blessed by a grateful church, his parents made generous donations to charity.

Hamlin knew God would always provide in times of need. He also knew it was humans who created their own misery. God was there to create the lesson, which was preached often, that bad things happen to good people. Hamlin struggled with the concept when his mother died of a virulent cancer, just before he entered National Service. It shook him. He prayed silently during training and in the war-stricken land where he served as a medic. There was no time for recriminations. At times he felt like a cheetah whose long lunch had been stolen by hyenas. He solved the problem like the cheetah: he found a higher tree.

The medical corps was an easy adjustment, as he had long been a volunteer with the St John Ambulance. He gained an acceptance he had hungered for and the strongly built fifteen-year-old found another interest, a growing liking for the opposite sex which became in time an addiction. Hamlin had no trouble in experimenting with his raging lust. Many older girls were attracted to him. His style of laconic, boyish charm, of honeyed words and praise, had unwittingly made him into a user of women. It was the one black mark on his life. He suppressed the mark, preferring not to talk to God about the subject.

His constant seeking of sexual gratification persisted into his career and his marriage, which perched perilously, like a climber hanging on by its fingertips on a cliff face. And like a climber falling because he hadn't checked his equipment enough, Hamlin also fell. He had failed to check the signs that were there to be seen. His sexual addiction was almost uncontrollable. He was like a man shovelling snow on a warm winter day; as fast as the man would shovel, the flakes melted, leaving the worker with a barely contained shovel of grey-white liquid, pointlessly persisting.

All of those thoughts raged inside: the money, the marriage, the job, sexual encounters past or in the future. Please give me a direction, God.

A dream came to him on that night of pleading. In the dream, time stood still for him. He was in a moment neither past or present. He seemed to be in a parallel world where he viewed himself as an outsider, standing holding a case, saying over and over, 'Do good, do good.'

He woke up with a jolt. He had been sent a message. He would ask Father Timothy for the answer. Deep down he knew what it was. It would need considerable contemplation and he would need stillness to achieve it.

2

Father Timothy Drew Kelly

It is with some emotion that I speak about the life of Hamlin Baylis Wells. As a father in the Catholic church in this city, I knew him before he became a detective. His family were great churchgoers. He grew into a fine man. He confessed some sins to me and I know he was considered to be a bit of a ladies' man, though he never let it interfere with his job. We chatted inside and outside the confessional box. I know him better than most and, more importantly, I know what drives him. He is a paradox of a man with an outer shell that many would find hard to penetrate.

He is now about to commence a journey and I hope it will be a God-inspired one. He still has more questions than answers. On the surface he appears to have answers, yet within him it seems another soul impersonates him, giving out glib replies, which satisfy for a time until the dragon once again arises.

In hope of a simple reply, I referred him to the story of the emperor's new clothes with its message that you should not fool yourself. He took this on board.

When time permits, I will discuss his life further but at the moment I am busy hanging onto life. I have bouts of the shakes and shivers, like all sufferers of Parkinson's disease.

Here comes my carer James with my medication. He changes the tape for me then nods and wheels me to the dining room.

Friends say I snore a lot nowadays. Maybe God snores. Why not? Or is it my snoring waking me up? Dear me. It's a question. God, Jesus, I feel you both near me.

3

Hamlin Baylis Wells

I confessed to Father Timothy all my sins, including keeping the money, and he listened very carefully. I outlined to him my thoughts, which he echoed. He concluded by outlining my options. He was sure I should not spend a penny of the money and would give me advice on its use. I handed over fifty thousand dollars, which went to a worthy list of recipients. We spoke about my desire to lead a more authentic life and what type of contemplation I might need.

I was retired by now and had purchased a twin-cab vehicle and a camper-trailer with my own money. The house had been sold and its proceeds divided. I was living in my dad's old house; he was now in Tasmania with his wife Angela. My payout from the job was good and I was now on a TPI pension from the army. Sex was still a problem to me, however. The blocking out of the past still lingered, and I found divorce blackened the goodness as I stumbled on in a single life.

I was lurching along trying to catch up to my mythical horse which was nearby. I was puffing against a tree, having galloped and subsequently fallen. Get back on the horse, so they say. I am trying. Slow the tempo, just be. The waiting might make me realise who I am. I am waiting for a pivotal moment. In the waiting, I have seen that my life-long pursuit of positive action and an affirmative result has become a monkey on my back

I have struggled with just letting life happen. I feared that laziness would be the result. I was missing the point. As humans, we must perform certain functions which make us secure, like collecting nuts for winter. An over interest in security had led me down the path of control and manipulation. Simplicity of life must come to the fore from now on. I had to learn that, even if we cease to exist, life would not cease. We would just go to another plane.

It's coming together. I have to conquer the sex stuff. Perhaps I can let myself down gently in my favourite area.

4

Hamlin Baylis Wells

So much has transpired since I retired from the force two months ago, the worst of all being my father's passing. His house will soon go on the market and I have reached the conclusion that I no longer need to own a house. The camper-trailer will suffice after the sale.

Father Timothy seems to be in remission. I hope so. I discussed the money with him and made a decision. With permission from the church, we would be joint owners for the time being in a suitable farm property. I asked Tim to stow the money until I return from my wanderings. The property would be self-sufficient in time, somewhere in the south-east. The main mission would be to assist homeless people with temporary accommodation and hopefully establish a boot camp for wayward youth. All the money would be used in the purchase and I am willing to top up if required.

I spend much time now contemplating.

I was at Dad's home a few nights ago making my easy-fix meal, still like the mainstream of citizens who require life to move at an accelerated pace. The TV was tuned to a US cop show, in which complex issues were solved within the hour. Unbelievable plots and dialogue so pat it was almost funny, spoken by phoney cops, either all goody-two-shoes, or on the take.

The doorbell rang and I guessed it would either be folk promoting Optus or evangelists. They would be unsuccessful.

I wiped my hands and opened the door. There on my doormat stood a tall thirtyish blonde woman. Pretty, striking-looking. I saw she had stubbed out a cigarette butt. My hormones had not forgotten me. And my first chakra was expanding. I greeted her with a smile while deviously making plans.

She held up a Bible. 'Is Jesus in your passenger seat?'

Novel, I thought. I replied, 'I've got a Harley.'

She was quick. Pushing back a forelock, with a breath she said, 'I see you have a fire blazing away. Is there room for Jesus in your life?'

I thought on that. Two questions. Was she suggesting Jesus gets cold? Would he like a rest in a warm room?

I gathered myself. 'There's only one recliner. The missus took the other one when she left.'

'Oh,' she replies. And then she holds up the Bible and says, 'What can I do for you?'

Quick now. 'Would you strip for Jesus?'

She looks flustered but recovers. 'I am not here to satisfy your lusts.' She lectures me on sins and Satan.

I close the door as she is speaking. I hear her shuffling on the doormat. A card is pushed under my door, which I read. It is a real estate card. Handwriting on the back signed by 'Cheryl'. Urging me to call her. Chuckling, I realise Jesus must be into real estate and, by the look of it as she drives off in a new four-wheel drive, some of his flock are doing very well.

Two nights later the doorbell rings. It is Cheryl. I smell her lavender perfume and no fags are in evidence. I invite her in and as I have a Scotch I offer her one.

She gulps it down. 'Can I at least look at the house?'

'Feel free,' I say.

She wanders off and calls out, 'Whatever offer you might get, I can improve on it. There are buyers waiting.'

I reflect on this and seize the moment. 'Let's get to business. I might be selling. Can you forget God for a moment, a long moment actually, while I couch my terms in a sensitive manner.'

'Go on,' she says.

'Let's try the bed out for starters, OK?'

Steady eyes bore into me; they narrow. She produces a contract and says, 'Sign first.'

Which I do promptly, thinking this might be the last one for me.

It was a great night. I like direct people. It continued till settlement. We became good friends. I look back with affection, cherishing Cheryl. I occasionally see her on those TV evangelist programs. Her last parting words to me were 'God works in mysterious ways.'

Having dealt with many addicts in my career, I was determined not to travel along that path. I knew there was more to life than increasing its speed. So why did I have to be doing something all of the time?

I spoke to Tim about it.

His response was as expected. 'Take that break now. Get going on the road. I'll be here when you return. God has given me time to help with our joint good works.'

I took his advice, packed up provisions, stored furniture, let Angela know and I hit the road…travelling north.

5

Hamlin drove off, not looking back He had seen an advert about a Buddhist retreat in central NSW. It seemed encouraging, with offers of solitude, meditation and a simple journey. He would give it two weeks, longer if necessary. He stopped on the way at van parks, chatting with the grey nomads in a relaxed atmosphere. He had no time constraints.

The gates to the retreat loomed into view on a bright sunny day. He drove in and saw a parking place. His vehicle was the only one amongst a mountain of bicycles. He felt slightly uncomfortable, almost like an elephant in a Volkswagen. He read the instructions on the gate before walking along the pathway.

Monks were strolling about, all muttering, probably prayers. There he stood in his tracksuit, looking out of place like a zebra without stripes. He was by now attracting some attention from the monks. Orange robes flowing about, flapping in the wind and bald heads and beady eyes peering at him as if he was a magician juggling emu eggs.

His pace quickened as he approached the giant house with its well kept garden beds lovingly tended by a mix of caucasian and Asian people all now smiling towards him, all dressed in work clothes.

A man ambling about in a dress suit seemed to be out of place and Hamlin nodded at him as he passed by. He watched the man, and his suit adorned with Collingwood stickers, his bulging neck and red face. He was seemingly oblivious to stares from people about. Even the monks, who he guessed would never mock the afflicted, were suppressing cupped-hand giggles.

A noise from behind and he turned round to be greeted by the obvious leader of the place, a serene-looking monk. The leader bowed and Hamlin returned the compliment.

The monk spoke. 'How can I help you, my son?' he said, his hands still cupped in a submissive prayer style.

Hamlin briefly explained. The leader was about to reply when the strange-looking man returned, ambling towards them.

'The man you see has been here for two months, always dressed the same. He needs a mirror to look into. I fear he won't. Not for his soul, but for his tight collar.'

Hamlin looked at the leader and knew he gave straight answers to simple problems. 'This place will do, it sure will,' he whispered.

The leader glanced towards the strange man as he made his way along the path, nodding to monks nearby and shaking his odd trombone-shaped head. 'You see, this man has suffered from acne all his life. His remedy beggars the mind. It consists of oatmeal, which he liberally applies during the day. It dries up, moves down his face and at this point he resembles a Christmas pudding. We hope in time he can see himself and overcome his fixation. He has free will.'

Hamlin tried to stop the laughter inside but finally it burst forth and the leader laughed along with him, both slapping their sides. At one point Hamlin fell on the ground.

'Do you see, my son? We are not all perfect angels,' the monk said as he helped the younger man to his feet.

'Well, yes. I didn't expect mocking in this establishment.'

The leader added, 'Maybe out of the mocking, which he has ignored, will emerge a greater understanding of himself. He may very well overcome his own trauma.'

They strode together to the house while the leader explained the rules.

Bells rang throughout the day and monks shuffled along corridors, making their way to meditations.

Hamlin waited in his room, his door open. The leader entered.

Hamlin stood up. 'Great leader, I am inspired already, inspired to change my life. What must I do to build on my inspirations?'

'My son, for the moment I need perspiration, not inspiration.' The leader reached under his robes, producing a shovel.

Hamlin stood there perplexed.

The leader pointed out the window. 'In the morning, go to that patch of ground and dig it up and plant these potato shoots.'

Hamlin was off in the morning, after a bowl of porridge, digging away. Digging and planting to the next meal and then returning to his labours. He fell into a dreamless sleep and rested his aching back. He awoke next morning refreshed, with the ache gone.

The leader stood in the doorway, his face expectant.

Hamlin helped. 'What did that prove, great leader?'

'My son, when you came to us, your thoughts were scrambled. They needed a direction and you created a patch that will be nurtured. You have done God's work. Life is simple. You found a moment and time passed by. If you have lemons, make lemonade. Do you see?'

Hamlin nodded, smiling, reality dawning in those words.

'The pace of life, my son, takes people away from the breath of life. Be gracious for your gift of life. Stop and think about it.'

Hamlin planted many more vegetables for the rest of the retreat. He felt his life, like an onion, had layers which had to peeled, and he peeled those layers. Layers which had trapped him all of his life.

The time came to part and the leader bowed, Hamlin returning the gesture.

The leader, smiling, spoke, looking Hamlin in the eyes with his piercing gentle gaze. 'We have found that abstinence makes the heart grow fonder.'

Hamlin smiled as he walked away, saying to himself, 'He knew my addiction. Saw the red colour on the first chakra, I suppose.'

Hamlin drove away from the retreat towards the south-east of the state. He would explore farms in the area, call in and talk to Logan, a detective with whom he had once worked.

It was a quiet journey, with times in the van parks talking to the folk, taking one day at a time, contemplating how he had been able to banish unwanted thoughts while at the retreat. He now knew he had always had a problem with confronting agony in life, burying the agony deep, where it simmered like over-boiled peas in a pot. He had forgotten the important things. The questions of how and when in his life he arrived at a point where greed in its many forms overtook plain needs. The retreat and its simple revelations.

He concluded that from then on he would be like a freight train without brakes. The engineer, God, would control the train. Leave it to God, as had been said many times. Hamlin had used a conduit supplied by God and he would use it many times. He had become numinous.

His meditations were becoming deeper and frequent. He kept returning to a dark place, a cave. The cave had a stillness he had never known. An unbelievable rest. Its lack of colour was as if the lights of the world had passed over the cave. Yet in the black void he would at times catch glimpses of himself during his birth process. It was if an ancient old manuscript had revealed its pages, pages opening without wind or momentum.

At the end of the epiphany he went down on his knees. With arms outstretched, he spoke. 'I am now your obedient servant, God. I ask for your guidance.'

6

Father Timothy Drew Kelly

'Do good, do good.' They were the parting words which sprang from my lips on the last occasion before Hamlin left on his road journey. He had revealed to me his secrets: the stash of money, and his proposal. The money is safely housed for the moment within the sacred confines of the church. On his return, steps will be put into place.

Much good will come of his decision to jointly manage and own a property with the church. His name will merely be words on a document. The church holds the property, and always will. He advised me of his intention to eventually divest himself of his superannuation funds, as he is self-sufficient with his service pension. In effect, he has made a covenant with God and there is no temptation which would make him spend the money needlessly.

Many good works were achieved when the original fifty thousand dollars was handed to me. Even then he told me he felt the money was a curse, and he would be happy to hand it all to the church. We just needed a plan, a majestic one which would be a lasting good for many. He had much more to consider about his life and its pathways, riddles to solve. It was hard for him. I saw a variety of expressions flooding his countenance on more than one occasion. He hated to be wrong or to be caught out, a trait developed in his battle of wits with the other side of the law.

A letter arrived in the mail while he was away. Its revelations spoke something of the man. He was at a Buddhist retreat and had solved many of his inner conflicts. I am a rather a strange priest as I have studied many religions and approve of many of the Buddhist ways, except reincarnation. However, we are all God's children and each man must make his own choice. I let it go to God. It is for him to judge.

Hamlin's letter revealed to me his plans for the property which he would search for on his return journey, preferably in the south-east. Run-down. A dam and hopefully a bore. Vines, vegetables, a dairy, and other produce, aiming for self-sufficiency. He would purchase about six six-man army tents complete with duckboards and stretchers. Build a shower block and toilets, plus an outdoor mess area.

It sounded impressive. Among other purposes, it would be for the use of homeless men. He would be an unpaid manager and instructor.

He suggested to me that young priests might be seconded to assist in the building and I sought permission, which was granted. I was as joyous as a child who first learns to float, or rides a bike unaided. The news caused within me some healing. I am sure that God had found grace in me and in the project. I prayed fervently to God to give me strength to see it through.

The waiting until Hamlin returned was frustrating in spite of my life-long acceptance of waiting. I hoped that he had found a property, and I was for a time like a fisherman who had battled the elements all night, only to return empty-handed. Deep in my soul I knew my fisherman would return, loaded with a catch…soon.

7

Five Years Later

William Wilkins, nicknamed Wee Willie, was a desperate, anxiety-ridden man. An addiction to gambling had made him so, and he constantly searched his mind in a effort to find a solution to his addiction.

He had not always been addicted. It had come upon him later in life, after his third marriage broke down. He was once a respected RAN cook, a job to which he escaped from a long succession, in early life, of foster-parents. The life had scarred his memory. The residue of some sexual abuse remained, most of it held deep in his subconscious.

He shut out the bad memories and after six years of RAN service, with some operational duties, he joined the Victoria Police and rose to the rank of detective in a short space of time. Possessed of a good memory, he was for many years a valued member.

At the age of fifty-five it was if he had fallen into a swamp and the only means to extricate himself was a small tree root, which broke off as he tried to avoid oblivion. At home, alone, he would frequently produce his service revolver and place it in his mouth. He imagined instant death. Inner voices whispered GO ON, DO IT. He would put the gun down and walk to the kitchen, which was bereft of tables and chairs, having been sold for another night on the pokies.

It hit him like a flash. Those years ago, with Logan, chasing a drug dealer who was on foot on that cold night in Brunswick. The dealer had just disappeared. Then later the man and another dealer living nearby shot each other. The man had a case, probably loaded with cash. Cash never found. Who had got it? Much speculation, nothing concrete. No witnesses.

Holy Hamlin had been watching the place sometime before, but heard nothing. Perhaps he picked it up? No.

But now Wilkins mused. Hamlin had bought the property down south. It would have cost a packet.

Wilkins probed into Hamlin's bank accounts. No vast amounts were found but he would not let it go. 'Holy got it,' he said to himself till it became an obsession.

He formulated a plan to discredit Holy. His old boss Edwards and partner Logan all went to the same church, so that would be a dead end. If there was a lot of money in the case, it would be hard to prove. His plan would involve his resignation afterwards. It would be based entirely on his account and a hint of corruption that the press would love. He would make an approach to a TV channel and sell the story to them. He was working out what they would pay him for such a story.

He took a chance in contacting Logan by phone and taped the conversation.

Logan listened then, his voice rising in anger, said, 'Let it go, Willie. Drop it. We don't even know if there was any cash in that case.' And then he then hung up.

Wilkins had not thought the plan through. He forgot about his conduct sheet, which was littered in recent times with charges of neglect of duty. He was a marked man and many of his senior officers were waiting for a chance to force his resignation. He had become a liability.

Logan rang Edwards after the phone call.

Later, Chief Superintendent Allen listened carefully to Edwards as he spoke about Wilkins. An officer was assigned to follow Wilkins while he was on duty.

'Get me a copy of Wilkins's log each night, please, Ted. We'll see if it matches up.'

Within a week, evidence was provided to force Wilkins's resignation. It was left to simmer.

Wilkins was feeling very proud of himself as he sat in the foyer waiting to see the TV channel manager. He was ushered in and related his allegations.

The manager loved a good story but he liked a bit of truth to prevail. He noted the man's twitchy behaviour but, intending to push the matter on, he listened to the tape. 'Look, you'll need more. I suggest you take your tape to the Chief's office and we'll get his response. OK?'

Wilkins thought on this, and then agreed.

'You'll get about two hundred thousand if the plan works,' was the reply.

Wilkins rang the chief explaining his allegations. He was given an appointment.

Allen sat in his office. Wilkins was due in thirty minutes. The tape recorder was in place inside his drawer. He had been told by an old friend from his early days, now a TV channel manager, about Wilkins's conversation and he had in return informed the manager of the fruitless enquiry by Wilkins. He told the manager of the inquiry Wilkins had instituted into the complainant and explained how he had also carefully checked Hamlin's bank account and found that no large amounts of money had ever been deposited. He spoke of Hamlin's good works since his retirement and of how he had given almost all of his retirement lump sum to the church.

The manager told the chief he would take it no further. 'He intends to tape you, you know.'

'Thanks, Bill,' said the chief.

Allen had told security to search Wilkins and if they found a tape recorder to hold it and advise the office.

Security rang. Wilkins was at the front desk; they had found a tape. Wilkins was not aware that the chief knew.

'Enter,' called Allen.

Wilkins walked in and sat down opposite the Chief.

'What can I do for you, Wilkins?'

Wilkins briefly outlined his allegations while Allen sat, occasionally leaning back in his chair.

Wilkins hesitated, waiting for a response.

'Now it's my turn. We're onto you. We know about your scheme, about your debts, about your breaches of duty, your approach to the media intending to make vexatious complaints – for reasons best known to you. I have copies of your logs, which are false. And of course I know about your attempt to tape me.'

Allen opened the drawer and replayed the tape.

Wee Willie listened in stunned silence.

Allen then pushed across a pre-typed resignation form and handed him a pen. 'Sign here, Wilkins, and give me your warrant card and gun.'

Wilkins's facial colour changed from pink to red. His eyes now glassy and cast down, he knew he was trapped. He reached into his pocket, pulling out his gun. For a moment he thought he might blow out his brains.

He stood quietly and without a word turned round and walked away, his left foot still dragging, from an injury which he had received in the rescue of a child. He said to himself, 'All good deeds become punishable.' Shaking his head as he passed by the star gate, he blinked as he walked out into the bright sunshine. Recalling old cowboy and Indian movies with Cheyenne indians saying proudly, 'Today is a good day to die,' he headed towards the twelve-storey parking station.

Hamlin drove the twin-cab to Melbourne. The supplies he required would involve a trip to the Police Association with the next year's timetable for the volunteers on his successful boot camp exercise for wayward youth. He would also visit his old boss, Ted.

Parking was difficult and he chose a multi-storey parking station nearby. The top floor was all that was available.

He locked the car, spotting some uniformed police about, and asked what was going on. He was told that a detective was threatening to jump.

He peered through the line and a look of horror came across his face. He saw an old associate sitting on the edge of the wall. He slid around the line and saw Ted Edwards standing about ten metres from Wilkins.

Ted turned, and their eyes met.

Wilkins said to Hamlin, 'Come to gloat, Holy?'

'No, mate. Come to help. This isn't the way. Listen to me for a while.'

'OK, say your piece, Holy.'

'Wilko, you think your life is all a waste, don't you?'

'You could say that, Holy. You could say that. I was always jealous of you. I did good things too but I didn't get any kudos.'

'It's the job, mate, the job. A lot of good deeds aren't recognised. I guess I was lucky. Hell, you got a bravery medal for saving that kid, remember.'

Wilkins did not reply.

'You were always first to put the money in the tin for donations, I remember. I saw you give a fifty-dollar note to a bashed woman once.'

Wilkins replied, 'I'd forgotten that. You were the only one who called me Wilko. I hated Wee Willie.'

'You were entitled to some dignity. I'm told you have a grandchild that you love.'

Wilkins listened, and then his eyes clouded over and tears welled, streaking on his cheeks .

'If you jump, then you'll miss out on their growing up. It could create a cycle like a ripple on a pond – a bad example which might be repeated.'

'Yeah, Holy, but I might not have a home for them to visit.'

'I can guarantee a home with us. You can get a service pension. All's not lost, mate.'

Tears flooding, Wilkins said, 'After all I've done to you...'

'Come with me. Your future will work out and if it doesn't you can find another building. But not today, OK?'

Wilkins's old police humour kicked in at the last remark. Hamlin walked over to him and held him and they walked away.

Ted sighed in relief, and nodded to Hamlin.

8

One Year Later

Wilkins found a new life. His debts were paid off and a small mortgage was placed on his house, which his son and family moved into. In a short time he became a changed man. He was sent to the Buddhist retreat and returned invigorated with a clear direction.

Father Timothy had predicted his own death and said one day to Hamlin, 'That old elm and I are slowly dying but I think I'll precede him. You know, I hug it occasionally, Hamlin. Dear me, I've become alternative, haven't I? I looked at its spring growth and it seemed to say to me, "When my leaves fall again in June, you will be gone."'

9

Hamlin Baylis Wells

We buried Father Timothy in June this year. He wished for us to be in our service uniforms and Wilko and I obeyed his wishes. The church was full of mourners and many uniforms were in attendance.

Wilko is busy with the boot camp courses. I am grateful for my life. God works in mysterious ways.

10

William Wilkins

The blessing in my life came with the Buddhist retreat arranged by my friend Hamlin, some time after my rescue from attempted suicide.

I was a different man back then, until the rescue. It was as if I was the lion and Hamlin was my Androcles, when he removed my thorn and saved my life, a life which had been shaped and turned into misery because I'd gambled away my future. I was a damaged soul when I walked away from Chief Allen's office. Discredited, no longer significant because of the choice I'd made. The last option. Its finality would obliterate it all, in one last spiralling plunge to the concrete waiting below with its porous surface to soak up the stain of my blood marking the instant when William Wilkins ended his life.

I sat on the edge of the precipice with one leg dangling over, thinking about my fractured body after the sudden stop. Would my son visit and identify my broken body on a slab? I pushed the thought aside. Old Ted, my former boss, was standing nearby. His voice was lowered.

Yet I could not look at him .My shame-filled face would speak to him if I looked, speaking without words, with my eyes cast down in humiliation.

I heard a voice I knew. It was Holy Hamlin, urging me, with his quiet voice, not to fall. I surrendered to his option.

Under the guidance of the same great leader who had ironed out Hamlin's kinks, I was given new direction in my life. The leader was able to take my thought processes back to the time when I sat astride the wall. I found the means through his mediations and guidance to achieve an objective view of emotions. We do not own emotions. They pass. Sometimes as quickly as they arise. The twelve-hour work day at the retreat, in which I was engaged in making great quantities of soup, had placed my former erratic thought processes into focus. It had cleared my mind and I began to appreciate the moment and smell the flowers, as they say.

Just before I made my final goodbyes to the monks, I was instructed to visit the scene of the old parking station wall.

'It is your last demon and you must face it, my son.' The leader bowed and then walked away.

I drove to the spot and parked, climbing up to the point and gazing down whilst I breathed deeply, speaking a small prayer then ambling away. How many other poor souls would have made the final plunge? I shuddered at the prospect, with circular thoughts darting in my brain of trapped spirits floating about.

I strolled along the streets of Melbourne which had been my playground in days gone by. I recalled my last words with Chief Allen and they filled me with remorse. I had never said, 'I'm sorry.'

Approaching in the distance was an old gent stumbling along in a walking frame. In the wild rush of humanity, rude people were bumping into him, their eyes fixed on their goals. Oblivious to the pain, the shrunken man ploughed on. He seemed familiar even from that distance, and I stopped, hovering in a shop doorway, watching intently the laboured progress as man and frame drew closer. It dawned on me in a sudden flash. It was Chief Allen. Older, hunched, bald and frail, yet still carrying an air of authority.

The core of my body throbbed. I breathed deeply, walking to the edge of the pavement with my lips mouthing a prayer. 'God help me to get this right.'

It was not my intention to confront the Chief but he was by now very close. When he was next to me, I spoke softly. 'Hello, Chief. It's me – Wilco,' I said, expecting a sour look.

He stopped and looked at me, nodding and resting his arms on the walking frame. I saw the clear blue eyes and the expression, with the chin thrust out, softer than I recalled.

'Come closer, William.' His voice was gravelly.

I obeyed and reached out, taking hold of his gnarled hand, careful not to squeeze it.

'I am so sorry, Chief. So sorry I let you down.' Moisture formed in my eyes and then tears fell. I wiped them away.

I saw his glistening eyes and heard his soft response, almost like a psychologist, searching for words.

'I'm glad, son. Glad you said that. Glad of your transformation. I know you're with Hamlin.'

I was not able to speak straight away. My mind was forming a reply. The words driven by my regrets finally burst forth. 'I created my own demons. They're gone now.'

He nodded vigorously, in acknowledgement of my long-held inner pain. Waving goodbye to me with no concluding words, he shuffled off towards the Police Club.

I had made amends and I had found closure.

The coughing fit which I endured afterwards, with the emotion of those few moments, produced more specks of blood onto my tissues. I knew that the cancer in my lungs was spreading. Too many cigarettes, and years working in asbestos-flooded ships. Perhaps that is my pay-back, and there is an earnest atonement to follow. When I pray to God later tonight, I shall ask for a little more time to wrap up loose ends.

My, my, I have come a long way.

Epilogue

Allen made his way to the Police Club and was met at the entrance by his old friend Ted Edwards. Pints of beer were swallowed by both men. Tablets were consumed with the meal, for both men were afflicted with the same arthritic joint problems.

Chief Allen had not adapted well to his recent widowerhood; his loyal wife had catered to his every need. It was harder than he had expected. His chat with Wilco was recounted in the conversation, causing tears to flow from both men, but there were tears of joy mingled with the sadness.

'Must be getting soft,' Allen said. 'God's not only on Hamlin's side, he's on Wilco's too.'

They did not speak about the old allegations raised so many years ago. It was no longer on their agenda.

'Ted, can you order me a cab with this bloody mobile. Can't stand the bloody things.'

And Ted obeyed, as he always did.

The Last Journey

Prologue

Victoria, 2003

Hamlin Baylis Wells, the fifty-seven-year-old former Victoria Police detective sat and gazed around the spartan room which had been his solace and retreat for several years. During those years he had almost single-handedly developed his vast property in the green south-east of the state. His energy, coupled with that of some friends and the admired priest Father Timothy Drew Kelly, had turned the land with its buildings, dams and accommodation for homeless men into a huge venture: a paying concern and a saviour for dispossessed men.

The old desk in his room was made of Huon pine. Many initials had been carved on its surface over the years yet it did not detract from the whorls and grain of the shining apple-scent wood, still perfuming the air after a damp night. Hamlin used the desk as an aid to meditation in his nightly chat with God. His gentle caressing of the surface revealed signs to him of foretold events. He had learnt that skill many years ago when he spent some time in a Buddhist retreat after his retirement from the police.

Yet on this night, with all of the deep abdominal breathing, the still and the silence, the occasional hooting owl, he could not overcome his raging thoughts. Events in his life flitted into his vision. Events which had been discarded, almost like a ball kicked into long grass symbolising a break from the past. He had thrown it away in his mind and replaced the old engine of absolute compliance with a sparkling shiny version. Hamlin searched his mind to find the ball and unlock the secrets deep within his heart, yet he knew the lustre of the sparkling new engine had faded and the events which caused the forgotten pivotal moments had arisen and tumbled over, enveloping his thoughts like lava sliding slowly down a mountain.

The fading of the new engine occurred when a letter arrived from a firm of solicitors six months after he and his friend Wilco buried their beloved Father Tim, the wise counsellor. The father was an unusual Catholic priest whose beliefs bordered on New Age principles and an original man with a conduit to God, unlike any other priest Hamlin had known – and Hamlin had known many over his years of devotion to the Catholic Church.

In his will, Tim had left Hamlin a house in Hobart. With the will came a sealed envelope. Hamlin fingered the perfect cursive words written by the old priest which still caused evocative moments every time he read it.

'This is now your house, my son, because my older brother, a defrocked priest who hated the Church, left it to me with the one proviso that the Church was not to get their hands on it, and so it goes. I have watched you doing God's work, even giving the Church your superannuation money to develop the property. It is your time now in the sun to leave the life of retreat and celibacy and forge another chapter. There will be a succession of young priests who will help you until the new replacement comes. If it is the one I suspect, he will make trouble for you because he is a control freak. But that is for you to discover. And to help with your new life I very cunningly snuck $50,000 from your super into an account in your name in Hobart just before I became disabled. Some advice: rejoin the St John Ambulance – you can build on your experience in Vietnam as a medico. Forge on, my son, and God bless.'

Hamlin re-read the letter on his trip to Tasmania to view his property. He checked with the St John office by phone and they told him they would welcome another volunteer.

The flight back to Victoria had given Hamlin time to work out his future and he knew Tim was right and also very clairvoyant because the replacement was a Father Ormsby and within a short space of time the relationship with the new priest was exactly as Tim had predicted: first distant, then sour, till disastrous became the byword

Tasmania stretched out its great green arms, which added strength to his resolve, yet God had to help him. He prayed that night. There were questions he needed to ask. 'Am I deserting your good works? Will lust once again bob up? Have I found redemption in your eyes after my criminal act in 1996?' He answered the last question himself with a form of justification: but with the money I built all this in your name, didn't I?

No signs came that would support the justification. He spoke to God once more before sleep took hold. 'Open the drawbridge for me now, God, will you? Release me. Redeem me.'

Wilco appeared in his dreams and said, using Hamlin's nickname from his days as a police officer, 'Go for it, Holy. Go for it.'

Hamlin

'Faith is the substance of things hoped for, the evidence of things not seen.' – Hebrews 2:1

'No need for changes,' I said with an acid tone.

The words slipped out without any guile in the presence of Father Ormsby as he prowled the chapel, converted with our labour several years ago. I stole an oblique glance at the priest, which is not my fashion, but now was not the time for a confrontation. Yet it was lingering in the atmosphere.

I saw a gleam of triumph in those micro-seconds when the syllables slipped out of my mouth. Those shifty eyes spoke a novel in that tiny moment – a novel with a beginning, a middle and an ending. The beginning was that Tim and I had been running a show which bent the rules. It was a big hint recorded in the glittering eyes which sat inside a fat red face of gluttony. The middle of the novel was laced with sub-plots such as heresy, akin to the Cathars of the Middle Ages who did not use a priest to speak to God, and paid a price with horrible deaths. This was no easy-going priest but rather a rules-dominated, ambitious man, a reborn Cardinal Wolsey, sly and scheming. A man who would, with an innocent expression, drop big hints to higher authorities, ensuring the downfall of the uncontrollable. The ending of the novel would be charges, an inquisition, a conviction without a burning, all with an ending of Orsmby on his way to his glory, a red hat for services rendered.

I imagined him boasting how he punished the wicked, yet leaving out his lack of humility. How he would allow a form of contrition, and how he would smirk as the contrite almost crawled back and sat at his feet begging to be returned to the fold.

My churning gut either rejected an emotion not experienced in years or adapted to the new me. In any case it was as tangible as a slow-turning concrete mixer and I had to find a way to remove the churning, which was growing stronger by the hour.

The die was cast when I saw portions of the scriptures plastered about in toilets and the kitchen, and on the paths leading to the tents. The cork was out of the bottle and the genie roamed about casting his shadow in all directions. The scriptures meant nothing to my charges, who only needed a listener to either empathise with their plight or nod in acceptance, hoping they could eventually work off their woes.

There were loose ends to tie up before I left for good, and cops hate loose ends. My life was at a crossroads: either stay or leave. I had to help the men before I fled. They knew my flaws as well. They knew I had a hard surface like a tortoise shell. They also knew of my soft underbelly: I could not let them down.

Age mellowed some of my old notions and age has given me a clearer awareness yet it is not all a barrel of laughs. It is hardship and hurts when our antennae send back mixed signals. I had, ever since I can remember, a set of options lying low. Some call it a fallback alternative. Those options have built my personality like a military map full of new overlays as the battle progresses.

Like the map, my overlays gradually fell away when the battle to overcome lust for lust's sake was won. The overlays had become irrelevant up till now. But the battle has been joined and once more the overlays are returning.

The overlay of God and his focus in my life is constant and has never been removed. He knew of my crime, which took up a fair space on my map and for a while I thought I had blotted my copybook until Father Tim set me straight on that issue.

I withstood all my early battles and in time found a policy based on significance which I have since used with my charges to gain their respect and trust. I never broke a promise to them, ever. That fashion sustained the whole operation here up till now: the walls are crumbling and one long blast from Ormsby will ensure that those old walls will crumble and fall.

A rule book was everywhere and the natives were restless as Orsmby addressed the men for hours on end and all he achieved was to create a good case for a cure for insomnia. Yet the blind hypocrite never felt the message coming back.

William, my poor Vietnam veteran friend, wounded in body and spirit, wandered away into the bush for a few days. We all knew he had a small stash of the weed buried out there. And it must have relieved his nights of horror.

Ormsby's spies, the two very young priests who did his bidding, told him about the stash. William returned, apparently calm, to be greeted by his few belongings placed outside the tent and a note: 'You are dismissed from this property. Do not return or the police will be called.'

I was enraged and went searching for William. I found him hanging from a tree. I did not cut him down; it was a matter for the police. I tried to say a prayer to God but nothing came out to calm my rage while I ran all the way back to confront the control freak.

I lost control when I approached him. I grabbed him by the collar and threw him on the gravel path and heard him wince as gravel rash cut into soft white limbs and formed drops of blood on his hands.

'You bloody moron. Call yourself a priest?'

He cowered on the ground with fear in his eyes and I resisted the temptation to put a boot into his ribs.

I yelled at him as he lay prone holding his cross and muttering gibberish. 'William hanged himself. Go and see, you coward, out there in the bush.' I turned and walked away.

I'm next for the drop, I thought, as it was witnessed by his two spies. Assault. Jesus, mother of God, what have I done? Gotta get something on him. The old cop in me returned as I searched my mind that night. It was my turn to scheme.

The Confrontation

Jeff was a former covert army intelligence man who had fallen by the wayside due to drink. He was a reliable Vietnam veteran who had had two tours of duty in the war-torn country. I banged on the tent where he slept. It was one of the rules to announce our entry, and we all obeyed it because it gave the occupants a sense of pride and respect for their privacy.

'Jim, it's me, Hamlin,' I announced.

I heard voices and the clink of bottles. No use depriving them of some privileges, as Tim agreed.

'Coming, Ham,' and Jim stepped out.

I had already nominated Jim as my successor. I felt he could do the job with the minimum of fuss. I gazed at the tall, rangy, former regular army platoon sergeant who always came up immaculate and stood tall. We were friends.

I started to speak and he raised his hand. I closed my mouth.

'We know. All the guys know. Are you pissing off then, or not?'

'I will soon. My time's up but I might have to face the music. Assault, mate. Bloody hell, I lost the plot when I found William.'

'We know and we laughed about it. Hold it, we've got some spice for you which might help. Come inside.'

And I did, and sat alongside Jeff and Graham.

Jim spoke. 'Guess what, Ham. The two baby priests were chatting away last night as they ambled into the bush. I decided to follow them quietly.'

I was anxious for him to continue.

'There was Fat Guts in the bush obviously waiting for something or someone. I found a spot and crouched down. The two babies stood either side of him and then pulled up their robes. Both had great stiff dicks. Fat Guts starts to wank them. I reckon he'd practised it a few times before. Well, they blow the beans. Then he pulls up his cassock and they wank him together till he's finished and then they lie down all cuddled up together, close like. Within a few seconds, Fat Guts bends down and sucks off one of the babies and then the other. What do you reckon? Not bad for a hypocrite with a rule book. I was stuck for words, yet my mind wasn't. It was racing and providence, or maybe God, smiled on me.'

Graham had also witnessed the affair and continued. 'I was trying not to laugh. It was better than any porn movie I've seen. Can you use it, Ham?'

I nodded. Then I spoke again. 'Look, I'm not against homos or bi guys. I've changed my view but you got it right, Jeff. It's the hypocrisy and I'm not in a forgiving mood about William. After all, he should obey the rules, which he expanded on without the consent of the Church, I might add.'

They were silent about that episode, which was still fresh in their minds. They giggled about my comment on the rule book. 'What are you going to do?' They spoke in unison.

'Leave it to me. I'll fix it.' The plan was already formed. I walked away and whispered, 'Thank you, God.'

I banged on William Ormsby's door. Hearing the usual 'Come', I thought a rude thought – you know all about coming, don't you? – as I entered. I leaned over his desk and he moved his head back, once again fingering his cross.

'Listen carefully. I have a photo of you wanking the two young priests.' I shuddered a bit at my lie.

He stood up. 'Lies, all lies.' He shouted, 'You're in trouble, Holy. Anyway, show me the photo,' he blurted out.

'No, I won't yet. Later maybe. But I have two reliable witnesses who saw it all and they'll make statements, of that you can be sure. Your time's up, dickhead.' I walked out leaving him blubbering and heard the clink of ice as he poured the glass of whisky he was fond of.

I cornered the baby priests and within seconds had them howling. They agreed that it had happened but what they did not know was that I had taped their words and Orsmby's. I returned to his office without knocking and played the tape. He slumped, defeated.

I had the last word. 'You're out of here by dawn, get it? Or the powers that be in the Church will hear this tape.'

He waved me out. I guessed his aspirations were dented somewhat and the red hat would become a pie in the sky.

The sound of bags being chucked in the car and the motor running woke me up at five-thirty next morning. I saw him driving away from the property – forever, I hoped.

The two young priests avoided my eyes for the next week until Father John arrived. I knew him from police days – he had officiated at some funerals – and we shook hands. He roamed around chatting to the guys and tearing down the scripture signs, which sent out a good message that normalcy would return. Jim assumed command.

I had some tears in my eyes when my last day came. After all, it had been a labour of love, with the help of many (and God). I thanked God as I walked around the entire property.

My last wave as I drove out the gate reminded me of how I had missed the confessional with Tim and how I made adjustments by driving into the local town on occasions for some free counselling from the priest. The aura of the property had vanished in the last few years and the chapel was almost in disrepair and virtually unused. I hoped Jim and John would restore it to its old glory with peace for all who entered her doors.

Yet in the end my guys had demonstrated their loyalty and combined with me in a protest about their treatment, despite the fact that the Church might close it all down. I was settled when I heard John telling all of the assembled men that it was to be a lasting operation in tribute to Father Tim and myself. My spirits were once again lifted out of the mire which took hold for a short period of time The battle had been won and the overlays faded away.

Tasmania, 2004

I drove via the ferry to the Apple Isle, as it is affectionately known. Some believe it was the mystical setting for Gulliver's travels and occupied by tiny people, but most of the people I met who lived there were fairly large, no doubt due to the good earth and its bounty. I guessed the footprints I had left in Victoria were footprints akin to those in snow and melted as quickly as I passed on, which I accepted.

My twin-cab needed some air in the tyres. I finally found a service station with a gauge that worked. The tyres were only retreads and I suspected that there was a bulb in the front one which caused a flopping sound at low speed. It occurred to me that I was like that tyre. The bulb grew with the thousands of revolutions until the flopping sound became louder, causing the tread to fall apart and motion to cease. My life needed another retread and a search was in the air.

A big part of my search involved a raft of thoughts with regard to certain beliefs held fast by religious zealots. I had had a recent encounter with one. I concluded that being a zealot or trying to be one does not create a spiritual life. My Buddhist friends spoke openly about that several years ago.

Obsessive thoughts about religion build an intensity in some people which cuts off the avenue to a spiritual life. Many well-meaning people equate their lifelong beliefs (created by thoughts) to the whole truth and nothing but the truth. They claim to be the possessor of the truth in an unconscious attempt to protect their identity, and if anyone challenges their beliefs they react in an aggressive manner. It is not so long ago when they would have felt justified in killing people who disagreed with their view. Some still do even now.

I had exhausted all my prayers of gratitude to Father Tim yet a shadowy presence nearby with the cold air and slow breathing told me it was Tim and it was corroborated when the touch of his old gnarled hand brushed my cheek each time I shaved. His reflection smiled back at me. Spirits are about and I have seen them, particularly when the air is full of static electricity and the thunder resounds in the night. That is the time when I am open to messages from beyond.

I rounded the bend in the street in Launceston and stopped outside the weatherboard house of my younger sister Angela and her husband Les. She came running out to greet me. She was a mirror image of Mum with her fair skin and her gold brown hair tied up high like 1940 wartime women. Her nails, including the toes, were done and the sparkling blue violet eyes smiled, much like Mum's did.

We hugged and I wiped her tears away.

'What's happened, Hammy?' Her voice sounded like Mum's, steady and low, with a husky sound like Peggy Lee, one of my favourite singers of the 1970s. 'Have you left the farm?'

'Yes, Angie. I'm re-inventing myself.'

'Heard from Debbie ever?'

'Heard she re-married and she's now pregnant.'

She sighed. 'Getting a bit old, isn't she?'

'IVF, I'm told. Her husband's a naval officer, high-ranking.'

'She always liked 'em with money. You were too good for her, bro'.'

'Sorry, Angie. I was too distant and of course there were the affairs.'

She looked at me and said just, 'Hmm,' then added after a silence, 'Be careful of that creeping back.'

We promised to stay in touch and I drove on to Hobart.

Sally

I had drawn up a list of plans and scratched them off as they were completed, such as stack the fridge, see agent, fill in change of address forms and all the boring stuff which I had forgotten. Within an hour I walked outside for a stroll and at the same time I saw the next door close.

There she was – a golden goddess around low forties, tall, slim with her blonde hair in a ponytail. Her jeans and top did wonders for her great figure. 'Hold it, Hammy, hold it,' I whispered. 'I've just got here, just fell into the business of meeting others and this golden girl is living next door, I hope.' Her King Charles spaniel, about to go on a lead, ran and jumped up with a wagging tail looking for a pat. I scruffed his neck. I love dogs and I once owned a King Charles.

I looked up into the big round hazel eyes and gulped a bit because my Adam's apple went berserk, bobbing up and down like a nosy meerkat.

She looked down while I was patting the dog. 'I see you like dogs, and he likes you.'

'What's his name?' and I still gulped.

'Chummy,' she said.

'Good one, good one.' I stuck out my hand and she held it. 'I'm Hamlin Wells.' Not using the full deal.

'Hi. I'm Sally Henderson and I know all about you. This is a small town and the Internet fills in some spaces.'

I saw for the first time her great goofy smile exposing very white teeth.

'You're a veteran and a former Victoria detective. Not all from the Internet, just nosy, and my nosy friend who took care of your garden for years.'

I looked at her once again with more control and blurted out an answer. 'I must catch up and fix him for all the care he did.'

'Nup. Old Tim left enough in an account to cover expenses for a long time. You see, I know about him and your connection.'

I wondered what else she knew about me and what Tim might have told her. It was probably a silly assumption on my part but proved to be right.

'So you might know I ran a homeless shelter for men in Victoria?'

She just nodded her handsome head and the ponytail bobbed along with it, as did Chummy's tail.

'Anything else you know about me?'

A Military Medal in Vietnam saving wounded under fire.' She looked embarrassed in that second as her face flushed pink.

'I suppose I should say "Aw shucks, it weren't much, maam."'

Sally giggled at my best ever parody of John Wayne. I was not aware then but was told later, when we became lovers, what she thought at that time: 'What a catch. Must be fifty-seven but looks ten years younger.'

Simultaneously I guessed she was about forty-two but she was forty-seven.

'Come over for a cuppa when you're settled.'

'Thanks, I will,' I replied and I watched her walk away with swaying hips and in that moment I knew my groin had re-started. Interesting, very interesting, and I added in a low tone, 'Tim, you old codger, you. But I love you.' My antennae were up so far I did not think of God at that point in time.

I had had virtually no contact with females in those several years, apart from Mrs Johnson who travelled once a month from the nearest town to do our books. We all fussed over the grandmother with the Dame Edna glasses and a welcoming smile who made great trays of lamingtons which were gobbled with glee. She was a member of the church and a nice lady.

Then it all changed when I left the mainland. There was my sister and then Sally all in the space of hours and both of those ladies acted as women should act, letting the male take the lead and watching, listening for a chance to speak of their innermost thoughts, because they are really smarter than us mere males. That is my view. A shrink once pronounced that I had a mother complex, whatever that is.

St John Ambulance

I strode into the St John's depot at precisely 9.05 a.m. Punctuality has always been my life and as a result of my previous phone enquiry I was sure I would be welcome.

I looked at the reception desk and saw a thin-faced woman, middle-aged with straggly hair, brushing away flies and muttering about the air conditioning. She did not look up yet would have known I was there because the door squeaked. I saw it was half ajar and reached back to close it, which I did with a bang, hoping it might send a signal that I was there. Yet still she did not look up from her computer, at which she was tapping away.

'Excuse me,' I said finally. (I like to be polite.)

At last she looked up and without a smile curtly said, 'Yes?'

I replied with a 'Yes' and waited while she thought of something smart to say but she went back to tapping.

'Shall I come back?' I said to the vinegar face of the woman, who glanced up.

'What can I do for you?'

'How do I go about being a volunteer?'

Without looking up, she thrust out a form, which fell on the floor. 'Fill this out.'

'Don't have a pen,' I said, now enjoying teaching her some manners.

'Never a bloody pen, never a bloody pen,' she muttered while she scratched around in her drawer and held one out.

I did not take it but asked, 'Is everyone in this office as rude as you? If they are, I'm in the wrong place.' Hell, I thought, is this the world of commerce nowadays?

The inner door opened and out stepped my old corporal mate

from the Reserve dressed in an ambulance uniform with pips on his shoulders. 'Hamlin, how the bloody hell are you?'

We shook hands vigorously.

He said, 'Come in,' and we sat in his office with the atmosphere in better shape.

'Had some trouble with Vinegar Tits outside, have you?'

'A bit,' I replied.

'She's not too bad when you get to know her, Hamlin.'

'Sorry, Brad, haven't got enough time on the planet to achieve that.'

He grinned and quickly browsed through all of my stuff then looked up. 'Very happy to have you come on board, mate. Are you able to do a quick refresher course?'

I nodded.

He looked at his desk calendar. 'Two weeks next Monday. Five days. Okay?'

'Yep.'

We shook hands and I walked out.

'Cheers,' I said to Vinegar Tits and – wonders will never cease – she smiled back, exposing a set of nicotine-stained teeth. Maybe that's why she clamps her lips so tight, I thought.

I strolled back at an easy pace, first cutting through into the CBD. Walking is a good time to chat to God and I re-commenced my daily ritual asking questions and waiting for a sign of some kind. The nagging one was 'Have I become a dinosaur over the last few years since I retreated to a celibate spiritual life or have I just made myself into an escape artist?' Maybe I should have a new name – Houdini rather than Holy.

And with the vigour of my libido over the last twenty-four hours I have to watch it. I don't wish to make the same mistakes. If it is to be lust, it has to be pitched together with love or the old demons will once again take hold. On my stroll I saw a sex shop but despite the challenge I dared not venture inside. There were many adjustments. One was that I had to re-start the email system but it was like swimming. One doesn't forget it.

I banged on Sally's door and heard Chummy barking. Sally opened the door and looked just as fresh as the day before. Chummy jumped into my arms as I walked in.

'I'll put the coffee on. White and two.'

'You must be clairvoyant,' I said.

I busied myself looking at her photos on the mantelpiece above the great open fireplace. Sawn wood was stacked neatly underneath. The whole house smelt of lavender and roses and it reminded me of Mum's love of the two plants which she nurtured with great care. One of the photos was of Sally in an army officer's uniform with a Signals badge.

'Siggy, eh?' I said.

'Yep, still in it. Did some time in East Timor.'

I knew because I saw the ribbons on her uniform. One of the photos was her as a bride alongside of another soldier, also an officer. Another was her holding a toddler.

She came in with the coffee. 'Good times back then, Hamlin.'

I sat down and said, 'Here's to some more good times.'

Amen to that and we sat and talked for some time.

'How did the St John's go?'

'Good. Next Monday. A course. But the receptionist needs to develop some bedside manners.'

'Margaret, old Vinegar Tits. Not too bad when you get to know her. She has two mentally challenged teenagers. Her life isn't a bed of roses.'

I immediately thought about my quick judgement and regretted it.

'So fifteen years with the cut-lunch cowboys?' (I had seen her LS ribbon.)

She smiled once again with that great goofy smile and it hit me, 'I think I love you, girl.'

She continued about the Reserve. 'Joined after Bob left me for an Asian girl.'

'He must be nuts. You're a smasher.' I suddenly thought I'd pushed the buttons too far.

However, she blushed and seemed to welcome the old expression. 'A smasher. Haven't heard that in years. It was my dad's saying. But thank you, Hamlin.'

'Did you and Bob have any children?'

'Yes, a daughter. She lives in New York. She married an NYPD cop, a gold shield detective in the 26th Precinct, Danny O'Day. He's from a cop family.' She must have guessed my next question and pre-empted it. 'Yes, one grandchild – Liza, a great kid, rings me all the time and sends emails. Not bad for a kid, eh?'

'Never had any children myself. Wish I had now.' I thought about a few concluding words. 'I am glad I met you, Sally, and glad you're close by. I hope we become very warm friends.' I gazed right into her eyes when I said it and her sly smile told me we were headed for a bumpy, but evocative ride. I stood up and shook her hand. 'Whatever happens, Sally, I've had no female contact in several years. So you must be gentle with me.'

She giggled and pushed me out the door. 'Go and do your chores, Hamlin.' She yelled out just as I was shutting her gate, 'Forgot to tell you – I'm off on a weekend with the Reserve. Can't get out of it. Back late on Monday. Can you feed Chummy?'

'I saw your echelon bag and your cams behind the lounge. Thought you must have something to do. Sure. I can come and stay in the spare room, if you like. Leave me a note of what to feed Chummy. I'll catch you Monday. I have that course.'

'Can't hide anything from you. Nosey cops. Thanks again. Catch you later.'

I heard her drive off the next morning and finally camped myself in with Chummy, who was pleased for the company. Except he slept on the spare bed and snored most of the night.

During the second night I had a bad dream. I was determined to wake from it and I shuffled my legs, with my toes touching each other so that any sensation would allow an escape from the dream of shame.

In the dream, I was thirteen years of age and had just returned from my paper round and gave most of the wages to Mum but unbeknown to her (so I believed) I had snuck some girly mags under my jumper. It had a fishnet style and her piercing eyes which gleamed into mine must have spotted the covers.

I headed out to the tree house which Dad had built for us but was stopped on the way by Mum and someone or something was also behind in a shadow and in that shadow was an old cigar box. The lid was half open but I could not see the contents. I seemed to be running away in the dream. I saw the interior of the tree house with scattered clothes and the cigar box was suddenly there. I was fearful that some crouching creature was inside the box. I heard a door open and I was back in my bedroom for a while and Mum sat near then, whisk, I was out once again about to climb the ladder when she stopped me and reached under my jumper, pulling out the girly mags. I hung my head in shame about the discovery.

She smelled of Pears soap and lavender and her hair was as usual immaculate. 'Time we spoke, son. It's something your father should do but as usual he ducks away when he's wanted.'

I knew this was serious and was squirming at what she might say next.

'There are bags under your eyes, son. You look quite ill, actually. Do you know you'll damage your growth?'

'Damage?'

'Every time you do that, it takes blood to replace it.'

'Blood,' I whispered.

She kissed me and left.

My days of masturbation were over from that moment.

As the dream came to an end, I looked in the cigar box and saw an emaciated version of me without any blood, pale and wan. I woke from the dream and realised that it was all connected with my possible re-entry into the world of lust or love, hopefully love. But blood — what a story to frighten any boy who thought to run his hands down towards his swollen member.

Monopoly

Our friendship blossomed after Sally's return. It grew over six months with new friends, dining out and new movies – I had not seen any for many years, and I realised how much they had changed.

We were not under each other's heels. She had a career in admin within the Reserve, I was engrossed in my ambo world and the time slipped away. My raging hormones sat quite still and under control after I took up t'ai chi with a local group. Although Sally and I did not discuss it, we knew our relationship was for keeps and love could not be pushed. It had to be spontaneous.

I say it grew over six months but within three weeks I believe the closeness of our daily lives brought about a need in us both which was focused and building sharply. My cold showers helped but that shivering, quivering style much like a hair shirt suddenly had an ending.

We sat at her small card table playing Monopoly and I was the banker. I picked up Get Out of Gaol Free and realised how significant it was in my prayers and pleadings to God about letting down the drawbridge, an ending to the self-imposed celibacy. Sally made a suggestion which I quickly agreed with. But I had heard her speaking on the phone earlier to Danny O'Day and I could not resist doing an imitation. 'I'm noivous already.'

She brushed off the poor lines and went on, 'Let's make this game unforgettable. Take off all your clothes while I go to the bathroom.' She left.

I stripped and sat with my knees up tight on the table with the varmit raising its head.

She returned wearing a flimsy nightie and we continued to play, with me casting quick glances at her beautiful breasts. She whipped off the nightie and I gulped while she shuffled the dice, which caused her breasts to jump about. I was in torment and the varmit was tapping on the bottom of the table. I think the spirit of my mum was tapping out a message. Be quiet. Two taps for yes, one for no. I made the varmit tap twice just after I'd won Mayfair and Park Lane.

Sally looked at me with her twinkling eyes. 'Come here,' she whispered in that Peggy Lee husky voice.

So I reached over the table towards her and in the process I dislodged Mayfair. 'Shit, there goes Mayfair,' I said.

'Fuck Mayfair' was her reply and we fell on the floor bumping, grinding and moaning.

My exile had finished and I was back in the world of love, lust, familiar smells and moments which I thought had been gone for good.

After a joint shower as well as another round, we shuffled back to the card table.

'Now where were we before we were rudely interrupted?' The great goofy smile which I loved loomed on her face.

I had to reply with 'Mayfair, I think.'

And we fell on the floor shrieking and laughing like banshees, rolling on Park Lane and Get Out of Gaol Free, with Chummy jumping in between, barely able to contain himself with the new smells.

I wondered if Father Tim watched and was happy for us. I hoped he would be because with his connivance and, I think, God's, the love of my life had moved into my being.

Goodbye to the past was a saying which circled around in my head since my relationship with Sally had bloomed. Goodbye to all those pivotal moments of joy, pain, love and lust and isolation from the world into a life of spiritual yet tough labours, but I congratulate myself for taking on that chapter, because the moment became important.

It hadn't been important till 1996. For me, before that year it was making plans far ahead for what I might achieve and at the end of the day, in one mad moment, it all changed when I made one of those pivotal decisions.

I thought all those decisions I had made in my police service were long gone, of no consequence – done and dusted, as the saying goes – but I was wrong. Brother, how I was wrong. They were not sitting in some comfortable zone within my soul just seeping away to an ending, or snoring gently like some old dog taking a snooze, dreaming of past good dinners or whatever dogs dream about.

Which moves me to one of my favourite topics – dreams and the disseminating of them – for they reveal much after closer examination. A dream came upon me from some unknown space and wound me into a web back in time to 1976. There had to be a catalyst which caused the sticky web to reveal itself from its dark quarters and it was the name Davies.

Allen Davies was in one of the ambulance crews and when we were introduced, the demon resonating in league with that name took me back in the past for the rest of the day. In his presence I could not get the incident or incidents out of my mind.

Allen Davies

Senior Detective Allen Davies was my partner in those years. We were attached to a team in which our immediate senior officer was Detective Sergeant Ted Edwards, a man who was straight, honest and fair and attended the same church as I did. We were friends with Father Tim back then. Ted had difficulties pairing Davies with anyone because he was disliked and because of his violence towards drunks and, more so, to his frail wife.

Betty was a downtrodden wife who only spoke when her husband allowed her to and I quickly formed a dislike of him. I was told by others to watch him. I saw how she flinched like a cowed dog when near him and the purple bruises were all over what limbs she dared (for fear of reprisals, I guess) to expose. Her mother had a late baby when she was nearly fifty and young John, the twelve-year-old, often stayed at Allen's place because the mother-in-law and father-in-law were almost over the hill. John was raised by a cousin and partly by Allen and Betty. He also flinched in the presence of his brother-in-law.

The scene was set for some retribution. If not for the treatment of his family, it would be for one of the many beatings he handed out to harmless drunks.

Just before I saw an event with a drunk, I had words with Davies about his family. 'Gee, Allen, your missus needs a good feed.'

'Nah, keep 'em skinny. They go off like a fire cracker that way.'

I knew the hidden meaning behind his foul throwaway line. 'Sorry, Allen, you're wrong. And her brother seems scared of you. He cringes a lot.'

He turned on me, shouting with his red face smelling of grog (paid for by publicans only too happy to get rid of him). 'Holy, keep your fucking preaching to yourself. Stay out of my business,. you God-botherer.'

We did not speak for about two hours until he stopped the car and jumped out with his arms waving in the air as he approached a staggering drunken man. He hit the man several times till he fell down.

I yelled at him, 'Stop, stop. What are you doing?'

Davies bent down and whispered something in the ear of the prone man, who raised himself and took a wild swing at his attacker.

'See, he tried to assault me.' He dropped the baton and kicked the man in the ribs.

I had enough at this stage and knocked Davies off his feet and there he lay in the blood of the man he had just beaten. Davies tried to swing a punch at me and I hit him once more. I called for an ambulance. The unconscious man was carted away and I refused to drive back with Davies. I just walked back to the station, giving him time to tell Ted a pack of lies. Which he did.

'Okay, Hamlin, tell me the story. I've heard his version. He claims you assaulted him and he has a torn shirt to prove it.'

'What do you think, Sergeant? Anyway, I refuse to work with him. I'll give you a full report straight away.'

'In the morning, Hamlin. Go home now.'

The phone rang at eight a.m.

'Hamlin, the old drunk made a full statement and the evidence backs it up. Davies has been arrested and he'll face court today. I reckon he's going down big time and the Big Boss will be only too happy to see him go. Even though there's some grumbling in the ranks, most secretly think you had some guts to tell the truth. But a story will get around and you know what cops think of whistle-blowers.'

'I don't care what they think. My conscience is clear and he beat a helpless man.'

I stuck by my story despite all the efforts of a half-drunk lawyer trying to destabilise me. Davies got seven years, initially because others came out of the woodwork. Cold cases were reviewed which made the sentence severe with a further stretch. He pointed an imaginary gun at me as he was being led away to prison.

Ted had a struggle placing anyone with me for a while and made a suggestion. 'There's an undercover position coming up very soon. Do you want it? It's yours. Of course you'll have to undergoing some training. Long hours. Debbie might not like it, though.'

His doubt about Debbie proved to be accurate and started our marriage's decay into oblivion.

Now I wonder, since the dream, if Davies is re-emerging to carry out his promise.

I watched the TV news some time after the dream about Davies and it all unfolded. Sally was on the phone speaking to Susan in New York and did not hear the gasp of the chair which broke and I fell on broken glass. She rushed out and saw me holding the arm up high, stopping the blood.

'Christ, what did you do?' she said as she loaded me in the car for the drive to the hospital. 'What caused it? Something on the telly?'

I nodded. 'Davies. Bloody Davies. You know, the one I whistle-blew on.'

'Yes, I remember. So what's happening with him?'

'I didn't know he got bulk time and killed a bloke in prison but got off with a short term – a sort of a self-defence thing, they say. He's escaped. Might even be here. Has friends in the bush and wears disguises.'

Sally went quiet but she sensed the danger which was lurking. The air in the car was full of enough static electricity to start a generator.

I touched the door handle and yelled out, 'Ouch. Remind me tomorrow, love, to ring my old boss, Ted. He's retired but he's always at the Police Club.'

They stitched me up, gave me some panadol and sent me home and I stayed at Sally's for a few days.

Chummy never left my side and stared at me with his sad eyes, and he licked my bad arm when he could.

The Next Day

'Ted, it's Hamlin.'

The voice on the other end was gravelly. 'How are you, Hamlin? How's Tassie? Heard you bailed out. Good for you. You've done enough for the community.'

I acknowledged his good words without mentioning my stitched arm, which was just the stuff of life. 'Davies, mate. What do your mates say about it? Is he here?'

'Good possibility, mate. He's a driven man. He even blamed you for Betty's suicide – she jumped off a cliff.'

'That was predictable, Ted. What about her brother John?'

'Don't know. Heard he went into the army. That's about it. Look, Hamlin, I'll explain your position to the Hobart superintendent and I'm sure you'll get a call from them. Would that help?'

'I reckon, Ted. Thanks. Like to catch up some day, mate.'

'You know my address, mate – either here, the bowling club or the Police Club.'

My thoughts raced back to Ted, who was as wise as our old mate Tim. And yet even Ted was reduced to wearing the bowling whites and the dreaded bowling hat on the tram. And of course still drinking pints at the Police Club, I suppose. I was loath to ask God for protection because it would have been a bit wimpy. I'm not some poor downtrodden bloke who's scared of his shadow. I also knew if Davies got within my space I would do my best to overpower him and if that meant killing him, I would, without any pangs.

The Old Copper was certainly back and God might not like it, because I felt the churning coming back inside my body which would not be resolved until one of us was dead.

'Good to see you, Shane.' I shook hands with the local police sergeant. 'Long time no see, mate. In Nasho and then to the police and you went back to Tassie with the police. Thirty years like me, mate.'

It was a fair burst for Shane Drummond to absorb but his thoughtful face took it all in. He was heavier than when we last met. After all, we were only twenty years old back then.

'I heard you'd left the shelter and moved here. You were always socially minded in the army. You did good work there, Hamlin.'

I saw a photo on his desk of two girls with an attractive woman. 'Yours?'

Shane's expression changed and he spoke slowly. 'Yes, but I don't see them. Missus took them when she pissed off with a Blue Orchid officer. They live in NZ.' He picked up the photo and fingered it.

I broke the moment. 'That's life, isn't it? Got anyone else in your life?'

'Yes, an ambo corporal. You might have met her. Word gets around.'

'So I've noticed. I guess you know about Sally Henderson. The Reserve Siggy Looey?'

'Of course. Great-looking lady and a good catch, mate. My lady's in the Reserve too. They have another exercise coming up soon.'

'Yes, I'm going as an ambo. I'm not bad at map reading.'

There was a pause for a while then Shane spoke. 'Davies. Your enemy, I hear. I've been told the whole story.'

'Do you think he is in Tassie?'

'Good chance. He has jailbird mates here. Some live in caves out in the scrub. Might be stocked up – there's always reports of gunshots about. Some stocking up on weekend meat, I suppose.'

I was not comforted by the cowboy words and looked serious, which he picked up. Especially after I spoke once more. 'Or doing a Milat, mate.'

That put Shane into a thoughtful mode. He stroked his chin. 'Look, I'll put the helicopter on standby before the weekend exercise.

You never know. We'll keep an eye on Sally's place as well as yours, which is close of course.' And he grinned a big cheesy parting of his lips and I grinned back.

'Of course,' parroting his words.

'Stay in touch, Hamlin.'

We shook hands and I left, yet I was not comforted because I had a strong feeling of doom.

The Exercise

I read the handout which had been supplied to each member. It was relatively simple. The map showed that the ground which the troops were to move about on was heavily wooded but reasonably flat and on that point I was happy from an ambo's point of view because I could easily manoeuvre if required to rescue anyone who might be hurt. The map stared at the eight people including myself.

Major Thomas asked everyone to read the instructions and at the end spoke. 'Any questions at all, bearing in mind some of you have never negotiated the bush with a compass using features and back bearings, though we have practised it endlessly within these grounds.' He paused. 'Two teams, red and blue. A corporal will lead each team of three troops. I'll explain in depth when we get there but basically you'll be about two kilometres away from the command centre. Each corporal will carry a radio. One compass to each team, with six maps in all. Rations will be supplied when you return to base, and make sure your water bottles are full. We'll camp out tonight with our hooches and you should all be home by 1700 hours on Sunday. Okay. You've all met Hamlin Wells, a former soldier and a Reserve sergeant in the Medical Corps. He'll park the four-wheel ambulance in the bush near where the map reading will finish. I'll drive the few kilometres to the spot when told by the team leaders of completion and that's where we'll camp for the night. Tomorrow will be some chats about camouflage and camp hygiene. Corporal, dismiss the parade after Mr Wells has spoken informally to the troops.'

Major Thomas walked off to his Land Rover. I noted that one of the corporals was Shane Drummond's girlfriend. The other was as old as me; nothing would be more boring for him than being on this exercise.

'Okay, this is informal but listen carefully.' I flashed up on a screen an old gaol photo of Allen Davies. 'You have no doubt heard and seen the publicity about this man. Trust me, he is dangerous. He has killed. Sergeant Shane Drummond tells me there's a chance he may be in the area. He's a skilled bushman and has some crooks as friends in the area, so it's rumoured. Be on your toes. I do not want to cart anyone back in a body bag. If you hear the slightest odd noise or see someone strange, let me or Major Thomas know straight away. I don't mean to have you panicking and letting us know about every noise from one of the Tassie devils in this area but I reiterate: be on the alert. We're not taking any chances and even if someone falls and is hurt, Sergeant Drummond has a helicopter on standby. Any questions?'

A pretty recruit about eighteen still with the smell of hairspray and deodorant spoke. She was almost in my space. 'Do you know this man?' Her question was quite innocent.

'I ought to. I was the man responsible for getting him convicted in the first place. He was on my team when I was a detective.'

That was enough and there were no more questions.

I took three troops in the ambulance and the major loaded the rest in his troop-carrier Land Rover, which would be used as a command centre. I explained on the journey that it would be a pincer movement, with the teams moving laterally towards a large outcrop of rock, covering a distance each of about two kilometres.

I arrived at the command centre spot and noted that the major had set up an annex and a base radio and his two 'chairs millionaires', as the army called them.

He looked like he was in for a relaxing time as well as getting paid well as a Reserve man for the weekend.

My guys took their packs and hopped out and as I drove off I saw the two teams marshalling. I found the rocky outcrop but drove on a bit further into the bush and camouflaged the vehicle just to be on the safe side. I radioed the major and he acknowledged. From now on it was just a matter of waiting while the troops made their way towards my location. It was a bright sunny day.

I heard the teams radio in that they had commenced and I checked my green old army watch; it was 1100 hours on the dot. An hour had soon gone past, yet I had not heard from the command centre (the major had stipulated teams were to check in every thirty minutes). Ah well, a comfort stop, I suppose. No sooner had that thought come to my mind than I heard a muffled cry from the command centre radio. It grew in strength and was alarming.

'Cancel, cancel exercise. I'm bleeding. Must have been a rock. All troops go to ground now. Just wait while I put on a bandage.'

There was total silence; I did not attempt to send a message. Alarm bells rang: Davies is here somewhere. And the old gut churned. I crawled out of my hide and heard the distinctive sound of a rifle being cocked

I grabbed the binoculars and searched the horizon and there it was, an outline on top of the rocks. A figure of a man lying down staring through the sights of his rifle and no more than twenty metres away. I knew he would have a commanding view of the ground. He would be able to spot any movement by the troops. Then the sound of a click from a trigger and a scream from about a hundred metres away. Shit. He's got a silencer. Then another with another scream.

I had to do something. He was just picking them off. I grabbed an entrenching tool from a rack and crept as fast as I could, silent as a stalking lioness, towards the rock. I reached the base just as he was slithering down. My foot was on the base and he was only three metres from me. He turned round and saw me. It was an aged version of Davies yet more bitter in his features than I could recall (he used to laugh a bit once). By this time I was on him while he was trying to cock his rifle. I struck down on his skull with all my strength and the blade edge hit him on the top of his head, thunk, and it split his head into two bleeding pieces. His eyes rolled back and I thought he was dead.

I kicked the rifle away and called Major Thomas and the teams. 'Come to the rocks. I've got him. He might be dead.' Not exactly strict radio procedure but I didn't care. I grabbed a huge bandage out of my kit and applied it in an effort to stem the blood flow and I spotted the grey matter pulsing.

'Major Thomas, can you hear me? If you can, call Sergeant Drummond. We need the chopper right away. I don't know what the wounds of the troops are.'

He clicked in acknowledgement.

'Blue leader to ambo. One bullet wound to the leg. Applying a restrictive bandage.'

'Red leader to ambo. A shoulder wound. Ditto.'

And it was over.

Major Thomas picked up the troops and returned to the termination spot, where a flat area was provided for the chopper, and it was not long before we heard that doca doca doca doca sound which still frightens the tripe out of Vietnam vets. Davies was still out.

Jumping out of his vehicle with a shocked look on his face, Sergeant Drummond drove straight to the point. 'Your lady's okay. Coming back now.'

I shouted and must have looked like a boxer who'd stayed for fifteen rounds.

'Jesus H. Christ.'

I squirmed a bit when I heard the blasphemy.

'How are you, Hamlin?'

'Okay, mate, but he's not.' I pointed to Davies.

'You've killed the bastard. Good riddance.' Yet in that dramatic moment he still giggled.

'No, not dead yet. Can you put the cuffs on him? Don't want to take a chance,' I puffed.

Shane quickly applied the cuffs and I heaved a sigh. I drove the walking wounded to hospital and left the surge of police now gathered to clean up.

Major Thomas thanked me for my efforts later when the hullabaloo had settled. 'Bloody hell, Hamlin, you'll get a medal for this.'

I don't give a shit about medals was my silent thought. Can't take them when you leave the planet.

Sally greeted me at the door and gave me the biggest hug but the great goofy smile was absent on tightly held lips and she held a screwed-up handkerchief in her hand. It had been splashed over the news all day and she sat in fear just wondering. We chatted right into the night because my nerves were so strung out I couldn't sleep, just like when I saved a wounded bunch of guys in the country, as the Yanks say.

The media was everywhere the next day and I couldn't move for cameras but I thought later on when they were gone, 'How did Davies get from Major Thomas to the rock within thirty-odd minutes?' He didn't look that fit to me but then I had bashed his head in so he wouldn't look like he was going to the mayor's ball, would he? I rang Shane and explained my thoughts.

He came to the same conclusions and yelled out, 'Jesus H. Christ' again.

I wasn't aware that the saviour had a middle name.

'There's two of the bastards. One is on the loose. I'll put a guard on the house straight away.'

He drove straight back to the scene and found a cave with two lots of guns, two lots of cam outfits and enough shot meat to sustain them for a month.

I gave him my opinion on the phone after he gave me the news of the second man. 'So it wasn't another Milat joker after all, Shane. It was Davies and his crony, who you say is called Sam Smithers. He's still on the run, I suppose.'

Once the guard was in place, we felt that a measure of normalcy and safety would return.

A few weeks later, Davies got a massive sentence, though he was a gibbering wreck after my hit with the entrenching tool. Our lives settled down and after a month the guards were removed. There would be no more nightmares or frighteners.

Or so we thought.

Two Months Later

Sally stirred the giant pot of potato and leek soup which was Hamlin's favourite. She thought about him a lot and, although they were firm as lovers, they would never marry. They planned a trip to New York and as the matter of Davies was resolved it was time to saddle up. She whistled 'Desperado' in between her stirring. She loved the Eagles, as did Hamlin, and he thought the title was made for her.

When Chummy barked at the door, she remembered she had let him out and the door was not latched. She thought about it and turned round: she saw Smithers standing near, carrying a tomahawk.

His long straggling hair smelt bad even at three metres yet he was scrawny and undernourished. His eyes shone like a man on a mission. 'Bitch, you're going to die now.' His eyes narrowed as he started to move in closer.

He closed in, carefully, as she said after it had all been done, raising the small axe. She breathed deeply to steady her shaking hands and remembered her army combat sessions. And never took her eyes off his his bloodshot orbs. At the same time she reached over quietly and grabbed the handles of the giant pot.

He was a metre away with the weapon raised when she threw the contents of the boiling soup into his face. He screamed and writhed, trying to clear his eyes, yet still grasped the weapon. She stepped to the right and stuck the three-prong barbecue fork right into his eye socket, making the eyeball pop out. He screamed and ran backwards, turning round and tripping through the open door She watched as he ran and caught his foot on the brick lawn edge, which threw him with force onto the four-foot picket fence. The fence was made of steel and the blunt points penetrated his chest He lay turning like a trapped fish, groaning and bleeding, and then he was still.

Sally breathed deeply and made two calls, the first to Hamlin, who was at the police station, and the second for an ambulance.

She sat down and lit a cigarette, her first for many years, and then the tears came, first gently, then in buckets. She sobbed till the sirens stopped. Hamlin raced in and comforted her but no words were spoken. The impaled body and the soup pot told it all.

Shane Drummond looked at the body on the pickets and said to the nearby officer while peering into the face of the dead man, 'Fuck. Don't take Sally on. She's not only thrown soup all over his face but poked out his eyeball.' He noted the three-prong fork lodged in the socket. 'I have never seen anything like this before even in the country.'

Hamlin walked out with rubber gloves and showed the tomahawk to Shane. The CSI officer arrived shortly after and the tomahawk was put back in the spot where it was dropped.

'Get rid of this piece of shit, boys, before the media gets here.' Shane addressed the ambulance man and fire officers who had started their portable saws. He turned to Hamlin. 'How did we miss this? How did he escape our net? Bloody hell, I'll have some explaining to do about this lot.'

After swallowing a couple of Valium, Sally's eyes were by now as wide as teacup saucers.

Hamlin

I was told, once the second drama finished, about Smithers. It appears that footprints showed he had scarpered to his secondary cave in the hills and lain low. He promised to Davies in writing with blood on a local paper that if the plan failed he would wait until security had gone and either kill me or Sally or both. However, his physical condition had lapsed after hard living in the bush as well as a bout of flu: his aspirations exceeded his ability and the weed which he smoked didn't help. The paper was found in his hills cave: REVENGE.

Melbourne, Ten Years Later

John Johnson woke with a shudder and knew his sleep was lost. Not that he cared much for sleep. It only came after a week when he stopped the uppers which kept his senses on high alert. They were needed in his mission of revenge against the perpetrator of all his woes. Irrespective of whether Allen Davies caused all of the woes, they were lumped together and shoved in John's inner suitcase with Davies the target. He had repeated the violent behaviour of his former brother-in-law and it caused his marriage to fail. The army had enough of him too and gave him papers which said in large print 'Dishonourably Discharged' and also proclaimed that he was never permitted to show his face again near a military base.

He sat in his room within St Vincent De Paul and scrawled out the plan; pages were screwed up and dumped until it became clear in his fragmented mind – just one more pill to stay awake, just one, and then I can sleep for a week. Might shit the bed. Who cares. I don't do the washing. My ex-missus always shouted about it. It would be easy, he muttered. Got no friends now. No one cares. Just a waste of oxygen, they'll say, after I've sunk the blade into his back.

John frequently visited the past and all of its horrors, much like a dog returning to its own vomit. He found no comfort in the visions yet could not escape from the technicolour which flooded his mind. Allen Davies, the once tough cop and now the violent criminal, who had got his just deserts a good few years ago, was released on parole, mumbling, hardly knowing where to sign the papers or how to hold a pen since the tremors of Parkinson's disease but his condition fell on closed ears to John.

Davies's former brother-in-law never forgot the reign of terror inflicted on poor Betty, his old sister. The frail, flinching woman with the purple bruises covering what square inches she displayed sent a message to even the dumbest kids that he was a wife-basher and he wondered why the police didn't do something about him. It took an honest cop named Hamlin to put the mongrel behind bars and years later the same honest ex-cop creamed him with a shovel. John wished that one day he might meet Hamlin again and thank him.

John remembered how, with his massive hands, Davies once broke a chook's neck just by bending his thumb over the top of his hand. John was eleven then. He turned twelve and challenged the giant cop after witnessing Betty felled with one punch, bleeding and crawling away like a cowed dog.

The wicked man sneered at John. 'Just sit, John, and listen,' which he did. 'You know how badly I could hurt you, don't you?'

John nodded in fear.

'And I will if you tell a soul about anything which goes on in this house.'

Whatever words Ted might have uttered hung on his lips and he just swallowed.

John remembered how Allen would calm down after beating Betty or issuing threats. The worst was when when he squeezed John's legs so hard tears came. In the moment the tears came, Allen wiped them away and kissed his young brother-in-law on the mouth. The taste of nicotine and whisky with its pungent smell always remained. After the kiss came terrible things that an older relative should not do to a child. From those awful moments John decided one day that he would kill Davies and it was stuck like an immoveable rock after Betty killed herself.

John crossed off the calendar as the day of reckoning approached. He knew where the monster lived and the nights when the carer would wheel him out on the street and be brushed away by the invalid who wanted to smoke. It was always after dusk and the smoking continued for at least ten minutes.

The black balaclava was worn as a beanie until he was within striking distance. His old sand shoes had no tread on them, nothing to point to the suspect.

John walked quietly up behind his enemy and pushed him forward on the chair, exposing the part of his back where the knife was to be rammed in. The old man coughed and swallowed tobacco. The knife was plunged in and twisted one, twice, three times.

John did not look back and crossed the quiet street, not hearing a scream. But he heard the sirens in the distance, minutes later when he was sitting on a bench seat in a park a block away.

Davies was rushed to hospital and the small item in the paper the next day said, 'Police are making enquiries. The victim is on life support and no perpetrators or witnesses have come forward.'

Davies

Dangerous Davies, the name used by the press to describe him, lay in a coma and on life support. The press had described him as a man who had danced through his life leaving in his wake a collection of fractured souls. And an eloquent TV journo built on the words with a narrative spliced with other titbits either scrounged from jail sources or embellished to satisfy the hunger of the viewers, who of late loved to be entertained by the life and death struggles of hardened criminals and all the muck-raking associated with their lives.

The journo made much of Betty's suicide and concluded that it occurred after a drug-filled rare holiday. They added that no children were left to mourn. The parents were ancient and in a high respite facility. No mention was made of John, as if he never existed.

The journo puffed and his eloquence continued. 'There came a time when death surfaced from his shadow and joined in the wake which had caught up and had overtaken Dangerous Davies.'

The journo could not know that his words had a certain ring of truth. Because Davies, although drugged, watched the comings and goings of the important people. He wished he could shout, 'I'm not dead yet.' There were no friends left. No one came to see him. He heard the sound of peanuts being munched in the next cubicle and an occasional fart bounced in the air. One was so loud he wished he played basketball and could slam dunk it, it was so heavy. He watched as the nurse switched off the machine and was alone thinking, 'No use, no use at all.' Then he saw a dancing light and heard an old voice which he knew. He thought it was Betty.

'Come,' the voice said.

'But I'm bad.'

'It's all over, Allen, all over.'

He felt a surge inside of him and blackness followed.

The Confessional

The portly priest sat in his chair taking confession. He yawned as it had been a long day in the small church in Collingwood, home of the famous Pies football team since their first beginnings. The sound of a closing door, followed by the shuffling of a chair being shifted, woke the priest and he looked at his watch.

There was a man in his late thirties sitting adjacent. 'Forgive me, Father, for I have sinned.'

'What is your sin, my son?'

'I killed a man without remorse. I stalked him and stabbed him.'

'Why, my son?'

'He raped me for years and caused my sister to kill herself.'

'Say three Hail Marys. I absolve you, my son. Go now.' He heard the door slam.

The priest shuffled back to his chambers with disturbing thoughts darting in his head. He poured a great glass of Scotch with ice which clinked as he swirled the contents. The tears came running down his cheeks. He had corrupted young teenage boys and knew in his heart he must pay. He wrote out a confession and signed it.

The ladder nearby was rested against the beam. He climbed up thirteen steps. He was not suspicious, ever. That was for Irish fools, his father always said when delivering blows with a cane to each child in turn till their backsides bled. And then he would soothe them. Yet worst of all they were all required to soothe him by stroking his swollen penis.

He adjusted the noose around his neck under the left jaw line and jumped off, falling about seven feet. His legs jigged a dance for three minutes until asphyxiation set in. Father Orsmby was dead and his face was slowly turning blue.

2014

Hamlin sat with Sally at the old card table where they once played Monopoly. It was the one and only time and the game had never again been brought out. They had spent the evening looking at slides of their trip to New York. Danny had taken his NYPD pension and Susan worked part time. Lisa had joined the police in spite of her parents' protests. They were now living in a quiet environment in New Jersey, where Danny wrote a lot and grew vegetables.

Hamlin washed down the blood pressure pill with a few glasses of red wine and never spoke about the dull ache in his left arm and shoulder. They watched the slides in silence and Hamlin sat forward when the scenes of Arlington came on the screen when he circled the veterans' monument and saw names of US medicos he had met. His digger's hat attracted attention and he was asked later to join the US veterans at their association, which he did. But he drank too much.

Sally stood and looked at him. 'She still looks good,' he thought. 'What a catch.'

And she must have read his thoughts because the same old goofy smile beamed in the same old way when she spoke. 'I've got an idea – not new. Set up the board and get your clothes off. I'm going to the bathroom.'

Hamlin was unsure if he was still capable of performing and sat with most of his clothes on. 'How do I tell her? She knows nothing much has happened for a while.'

The shower ran for a long time and then he heard a thud followed by a groan. His steps echoed with his dash on the newly laid tiles which had replaced the old carpet.

There she was sprawled, ungainly with blood seeping into her hair and with her eyes wide open. He felt her pulse and it was silent as her breath. Here was the reality of death, which was a constant companion for him in his life, always skulking, letting him know all those years, hey, this is temporary.

Hamlin let out a scream and looked upwards. 'Why, God, why? Why not me?'

He was in turmoil, holding his hand over his eyes and then came that old booming voice from above not heard since his days in the retreat.

'I have found grace in you, Hamlin. Sit back, be still. Your new journey begins.'

Hamlin always trusted in God and he obeyed, holding Sally's draped arm.

The sharp pain struck him in the centre of his chest. It was so sharp it took his breath. He gasped a few seconds and was still. He looked down from the ceiling and saw Sally's spirit rising, looking a bit bemused and brushing her hair back over her ears like she always did. She looked up and saw him waiting and the goofy smile lit up her whole face. As they moved upwards holding hands on the trip, they heard a noise from behind. And there was Chummy, who ran up and jumped into their arms with his tail wagging furiously, and they both kissed him.

'Thank you, God.' Hamlin's face still had the smears of the dried tears.

'Not a problem,' said the booming voice. 'Get in the queue.'

Epilogue

New Jersey, USA

Susan

'For most of your life you've lived as the effect of your experiences. Now you are invited to be the cause of them.' – Neale Donald Walsch

I stand here gazing at the horizon with Danny and we think of the shock which occurred when we were told the news. I have read the story of Hamlin Baylis Wells from the folder given to us by his sister Angela and it occurred to me that my mum Sally had found a great love at last, which filled the void in her life.

Our thoughts flood back to the two coffins side by side in the small chapel in Hobart. They were draped with the flag and the medals which both of them had earned. Mum had served in East Timor for six months. There were uniforms right through the crowd. Not in the least was Danny in his NYPD outfit, with Liza in matching gear.

Many people, including a senior priest, spoke about Hamlin's generosity in establishing the property in Victoria and in attendance were Father John and Jim who now run the show, which still grows in its care for homeless men. Various police came forward from his early days up till his last dramas and then of course Mum had many speakers. And then the button was pressed and that was it, apart from the music like 'Desperados' from the Eagles and 'I Still Call Australia Home'. Later on, their ashes were mingled and cast into the Derwent River.

I finger their medals and remember my first meeting with Hamlin. The instant rapport with Danny and the gazing admiration from Liza who secretly wanted to be a cop.

The brotherhood of cops is sustained and I know all about it. I knew they were both happy. And seriously in love.

I will grieve for some time, I think, but what a way for lovers to go. God bless you both. You are not forgotten.